LUCY (8)   CLYDE (11)   LINCOLN (11)

LENI (16)   LORI (17)   BOBBY (17)

LILY (15 mos) LISA (4) LOLA (6) LANA

LYNN (13) LUAN (14) LUNA (15)

THE LOUD HOUSE

#7 "THE STRUGGLE IS REAL"

PAPERCUTZ
New York

THE LOUD HOUSE

#7 "THE STRUGGLE IS REAL"

nickelodeon™ THE LOUD HOUSE #7 "THE STRUGGLE IS REAL"

"BUSINESS CENTS"
Angela Entzminger—Writer, Artist
Ronda Pattison—Colorist
Wilson Ramos Jr.—Letterer

"PREP TALK"
Derek Fridolfs—Writer
Angela Zhang—Artist
Ronda Pattison—Colorist
Wilson Ramos Jr.—Letterer

"UNDER REMOTE CONTROL"
Andrew Brooks—Writer
Angela Zhang—Artist
Ronda Pattison—Colorist
Wilson Ramos Jr.—Letterer

"GAME OVER"
Derek Fridolfs—Writer
Gizelle Orbino—Artist, Colorist
Wilson Ramos Jr.—Letterer

"FLIPPING THE SCRIPT"
Andrew Brooks—Writer
Gizelle Orbino—Artist, Colorist
Wilson Ramos Jr.—Letterer

"I'M WITH THE BAND"
Angela Entzminger—Writer
Lee-Roy Lahey—Penciler
Zazo Aguiar—Inker, Colorist
Wilson Ramos Jr.—Letterer

"FACE VALUE"
Andrew Brooks—Writer, Artist, Colorist
Wilson Ramos Jr.—Letterer

"IMPROMPTOOT CONCERT"
Derek Fridolfs—Writer
Melissa Kleynowski—Penciler
Zazo Aguiar—Inker, Colorist
Wilson Ramos Jr.—Letterer

"CRUMBINAL JUSTICE"
Andrew Brooks—Writer
Erin Hyde—Artist, Colorist
Wilson Ramos Jr.—Letterer

"LOW ACHIEVEMENT"
Derek Fridolfs—Writer
Gizelle Orbino—Artist, Colorist, Letterer

"THE LOUD HOUSE GAMES!"
Brian Smith—Writer, Artist, Colorist
Wilson Ramos Jr.—Letterer

"FIND OF THE CENTURY"
Angela Entzminger—Writer
Colton Davis—Artist
Gabrielle Dolbey—Colorist
Wilson Ramos Jr.—Letterer

"A MONSTER PLAN"
Derek Fridolfs—Writer
Angela Zhang—Artist
Ronda Pattison—Colorist
Wilson Ramos Jr.—Letterer

"OUT OF TUNE"
Andrew Brooks—Writer
Daniela Rodriguez—Artist
Erin Hyde—Colorist
Wilson Ramos Jr.—Letterer

"DEUCES WILD!"
Chris Savino, Karla Sakas Shropshire—Writers
Miguel Puga, Jared Morgan, Chris Savino, Jordan Rosato—Artists, Letterers
Amanda Rynda—Colorist

Cover by THE LOUD HOUSE DESIGN TEAM
JAMES SALERNO —Sr. Art Director/Nickelodeon
JAYJAY JACKSON—Design
ASHLEY KLIMENT, SEAN GANTKA, ANGELA ENTZMINGER, DANA CLUVERIUS, MOLLIE FREILICH, AMANDA RYNDA—Special Thanks
JEFF WHITMAN—Editor
KARR ANTUNES—Editorial Intern
JOAN HILTY — Comics Editor/Nickelodeon
JIM SALICRUP
Editor-in-Chief

ISBN: 978-1-6299-1797-9 paperback edition
ISBN: 978-1-6299-1796-2 hardcover edition

Papercutz books may be purchased for business or promotional use. For information on bulk purchases please contact Macmillan Corporate and Premium Sales Department at (800) 221-7945 x5442.

Printed in China
August 2019

Distributed by Macmillan
First Printing

MEET THE LOUD FAMILY

and friends!

LINCOLN LOUD
THE MIDDLE CHILD (11)

At 11 years old, Lincoln is the middle child, with five older sisters and five younger sisters. He has learned that surviving the Loud household means staying a step ahead. He's the man with a plan, always coming up with a way to get what he wants or deal with a problem, even if things inevitably go wrong. Being the only boy comes with some perks. Lincoln gets his own room – even if it's just a converted linen closet. On the other hand, being the only boy also means he sometimes gets a little too much attention from his sisters. They mother him, tease him, and use him as the occasional lab rat or fashion show participant. Lincoln's sisters may drive him crazy, but he loves them and is always willing to help out if they need him.

LORI LOUD
THE OLDEST (17)

As the first-born child of the Loud Clan, Lori sees herself as the boss of all her siblings. She feels she's paved the way for them and deserves extra respect. Her signature traits are rolling her eyes, texting her boyfriend, Bobby, and literally saying "literally" all the time. Because she's the oldest and most experienced sibling, Lori can be a great ally, so it pays to stay on her good side, especially since she can drive.

LENI LOUD
THE FASHIONISTA (16)

Leni spends most of her time designing outfits and accessorizing. She always falls for Luan's pranks, and sometimes walks into walls when she's talking (she's not great at doing two things at once). Leni might be flighty, but she's the sweetest of the Loud siblings and truly has a heart of gold (even though she's pretty sure it's a heart of blood).

LUNA LOUD
THE ROCK STAR (15)

Luna is loud, boisterous and freewheeling, and her energy is always cranked to 11. She thinks about music so much that she even talks in song lyrics. On the off-chance she doesn't have her guitar with her, everything can and will be turned into a musical instrument. You can always count on Luna to help out, and she'll do most anything you ask, as long as you're okay with her supplying a rocking guitar accompaniment.

LUAN LOUD
THE JOKESTER (14)

Luan's a standup comedienne who provides a nonstop barrage of silly puns. She's big on prop comedy too – squirting flowers and whoopee cushions – so you have to be on your toes whenever she's around. She loves to pull pranks and is a really good ventriloquist – she is often found doing bits with her dummy, Mr. Coconuts. Luan never lets anything get her down; to her, laughter IS the best medicine.

EL DIABLO

HOPS

LYNN LOUD
THE ATHLETE (13)

Lynn is athletic and full of energy and is always looking for a teammate. With her, it's all sports all the time. She'll turn anything into a sport. Putting away eggs? Jump shot! Score! Cleaning up the eggs? Slap shot! Score! Lynn is very competitive, but despite her competitive nature, she always tries to just have a good time.

LUCY LOUD
THE EMO (8)

You can always count on Lucy to give the morbid point of view in any given situation. She is obsessed with all things spooky and dark – funerals, vampires, séances, and the like. She wears mostly black and writes moody poetry. She's usually quiet and keeps to herself. Lucy has a way of mysteriously appearing out of nowhere, and try as they might, her siblings never get used to this.

LOLA LOUD
THE BEAUTY QUEEN (6)

Lola could not be more different from her twin sister, Lana. She's a pageant powerhouse whose interests include glitter, photo shoots, and her own beautiful, beautiful face. But don't let her cute, gap-toothed smile fool you; underneath all the sugar and spice lurks a Machiavellian mastermind. Whatever Lola wants, Lola gets – or else. She's the eyes and ears of the household and never resists an opportunity to tattle on troublemakers. But if you stay on Lola's good side, you've got yourself a fierce ally – and a lifetime supply of free makeovers.

LANA LOUD
THE TOMBOY (6)

Lana is the rough-and-tumble sparkplug counterpart to her twin sister, Lola. She's all about reptiles, mud pies, and muffler repair. She's the resident Ms. Fix-it and is always ready to lend a hand – the dirtier the job, the better. Need your toilet unclogged? Snake fed? Back-zit popped? Lana's your gal. All she asks in return is a little A-B-C gum, or a handful of kibble (she often sneaks it from the dog bowl).

LISA LOUD
THE GENIUS (4)

Lisa is smarter than the rest of her siblings combined. She'll most likely be a rocket scientist, or a brain surgeon, or an evil genius who takes over the world. Lisa spends most of her time working in her lab (the family has gotten used to the explosions), and says her research leaves little time for frivolous human pursuits like "playing" or "getting haircuts." That said, she's always there to help with a homework question, or to explain why the sky is blue, or to point out the structural flaws in someone's pillow fort. Lisa says it's the least she can do for her favorite test subjects, er, siblings.

LILY LOUD
THE BABY (15 MONTHS)

Lily is a giggly, drooly, diaper-ditching free spirit, affectionately known as "the poop machine." You can't keep a nappy on this kid – she's like a teething Houdini. But even when Lily's running wild, dropping rancid diaper bombs, or drooling all over the remote, she always brings a smile to everyone's face (and a clothespin to their nose). Lily is everyone's favorite little buddy, and the whole family loves her unconditionally.

CHARLES

WALT

CLIFF

GEO

RITA LOUD

Mother to the eleven Loud kids, Mom (Rita Loud) wears many different hats. She's a chauffeur, homework-checker and barf-cleaner-upper all rolled into one. She's always there for her kids and ready to jump into action during a crisis, whether it's a fight between the twins or Leni's missing shoe. When she's not chasing the kids around or at her day job as a dental hygienist, Mom pursues her passion: writing. She also loves taking on house projects and is very handy with tools (guess that's where Lana gets it from). Between writing, working and being a mom, her days are always hectic but she wouldn't have it any other way.

LYNN LOUD SR.

Dad (Lynn Loud Sr.) is a fun-loving, upbeat aspiring chef. A kid-at-heart, he's not above taking part in the kids' zany schemes. In addition to cooking, Dad loves his van, playing the cowbell and making puns. Before meeting Mom, Dad spent a semester in England and has been obsessed with British culture ever since – and sometimes "accidentally" slips into a British accent. When Dad's not wrangling the kids, he's pursuing his dream of opening his own restaurant where he hopes to make his "Lynn-sagnas" world-famous.

CLYDE McBRIDE
THE BEST FRIEND (11)

Clyde is Lincoln's partner in crime. He's always willing to go along with Lincoln's crazy schemes (even if he sees the flaws in them up-front). Lincoln and Clyde are two peas in a pod and share pretty much all of the same tastes in movies, comics, TV shows, toys—you name it. As an only child, Clyde envies Lincoln—how cool would it be to always have siblings around to talk to? But since Clyde spends so much time at the Loud household, he's almost an honorary sibling anyway.

ZACH GURDLE

Zach is a self-admitted nerd who's obsessed with aliens and conspiracy theories. He lives between a freeway and a circus, so the chaos of the Loud House doesn't faze him. He and Rusty occasionally butt heads, but deep down, it's all love.

RUSTY SPOKES

Rusty is a self-proclaimed ladies' man who's always the first to dish out girl advice—even though he's never been on an actual date. His dad owns a suit rental service, so occasionally Rusty can hook the gang up with some dapper duds—just as long as no one gets anything dirty.

LIAM

Liam is an enthusiastic, sweet-natured farm boy full of down-home wisdom. He loves hanging out with his Mee Maw, wrestling his prize pig Virginia, and sharing his farm-to-table produce with the rest of the gang.

VIRGINIA

STELLA

Stella, 11, is a quirky, carefree girl who's new to Royal Woods. She has tons of interests, like trying on wigs, playing laser tag, eating curly fries, and hanging with her friends. But what she loves the most is tech — she always wants to dismantle electronics and put them back together again.

SAM SHARP

SULLY

MAZZY

LUNA'S BANDMATES

"BUSINESS CENTS"

ALRIGHT, CLASS! EACH OF YOU WILL BE WORKING WITH YOUR PARTNERS TO CREATE A BUSINESS FOR THE SCHOOL'S *YOUNG ENTREPRENEURS FAIR.*

YES, *MRS. JOHNSON!*

CLYDE, WE HAVE TO TOP OUR *CLINCOLN McCLOUD* DELIVERY SERVICE FROM LAST YEAR.

OUR SECRET WAS UNBEATABLE PRICES THROUGHOUT ROYAL WOODS.

THAT WILL BE TOUGH TO BEAT, *LINCOLN.*

MRS. J, CAN I WORK WITH MY BOYS *ZACH* AND *LIAM* AGAIN THIS YEAR?

AS LONG AS YOU PROMISE THERE WILL BE NO SHENANIGANS, *RUSTY.*

I DON'T WANT TO RELIVE THE...

...‡SHUDDER‡ *SPECIALTY TOFFEE* INCIDENT.

HEY, TARTAR SAUCE IS A GREAT INGREDIENT! SOCIETY DOESN'T APPRECIATE *AVANT GARDE* PALATES.

THAT'S WHAT YOU'RE CALLING IT NOW?

TARNATION! IT TOOK ME *WEEKS* TO GET THAT SMELL OUTTA MY HAIR.

STELLA, WANT TO JOIN OUR GROUP?

WITH YOUR *DIAGRAMMING SKILLS* WE'LL HAVE THE BEST PROJECT IN CLASS.

COUNT ME IN!

BOOM!

BUMP   BUMP

12

14

"PREP TALK"

16

"UNDER REMOTE CONTROL"

19

"GAME OVER"

22

"FLIPPING THE SCRIPT"

"I'M WITH THE BAND"

"FACE VALUE"

"CRUMBINAL JUSTICE"

36

"LOW ACHIEVEMENT"

45

"FIND OF THE CENTURY"

THIS IS THE GREATEST DISCOVERY IN THE ENTIRE--

GREETINGS, SIBLING AND CANINE COMPANION.

LISA, CHECK IT OUT! WE DISCOVERED A *DINOSAUR* FOSSIL!

WELL TECHNICALLY TURKEYS ARE RELATIVES TO DINOSAURS, SINCE THEY ARE DESCENDANTS.

YOU MEAN, IT'S *NOT* A DINO BONE?

NO, THIS IS *MELEAGRIS GALLOPAVO.* STREET NAME: DOMESTIC *TURKEY.*

ERGO: LAST THURSDAY'S DINNER.

FATHER'S EXTRA CRISPY RECIPE.

OH, WELL. IT'S STILL A DISCOVERY TO US!

COME ON, BOY, LET'S SEE IF WE CAN DIG UP ANY *SIDE DISHES!*

ARF!

END

"A MONSTER PLAN"

51

"Out of Tune"

55

WATCH OUT FOR PAPERCUTZ™

Welcome to the sisters-surviving seventh, super-fun THE LOUD HOUSE graphic novel, "The Struggle is Real," from Papercutz – those hard-working residents of THE QUIET (publishing) HOUSE dedicated to publishing great graphic novels for all ages. I'm Jim Salicrup, Editor-in-Chief and Lily's Diaper-Changer, here with good news for those of you who just discovered that Papercutz is publishing THE LOUD HOUSE graphic novels…

But before we get to that, we just can't keep our mouths shut a moment longer about the really, really exciting news regarding THE LOUD HOUSE. We're just too excited! It was recently announced that Nickelodeon will be producing an original THE LOUD HOUSE animated movie for Netflix! That's right – a movie, featuring Lincoln Loud; his ten sisters, Lori, Leni, Luna, Luan, Lynn, Lucy, Lola, Lana, Lisa, and Lily; his parents, Rita and Lynn Sr.; their pets, and all their many friends! We haven't been this excited since we heard about that other upcoming THE LOUD HOUSE event, the new LOS CASAGRANDES series!

But back to THE LOUD HOUSE graphic novels… Since this is the seventh graphic novel of THE LOUD HOUSE, we're sure you've been able to deduce that there must have been six previous THE LOUD HOUSE graphic novels. That's 100% correct! If you've been picking them up at your favorite bookseller or library, and you already have all seven of the THE LOUD HOUSE, graphic novels then you're completely up-to-speed. But if you're just joining us, and feel a tad overwhelmed at having to find six previous graphic novels to enjoy all THE LOUD HOUSE comics that exist, we've got some good news to wipe away all your anxiety! Papercutz started a series of THE LOUD HOUSE 3 IN 1 graphic novels that collect three of the original graphic novels into one. So, you can find THE LOUD HOUSE #1-3 in THE LOUD HOUSE 3 IN 1 #1, and THE LOUD HOUSE #4-6 in (wait for it…) THE LOUD HOUSE 3 IN 1 #2! It's simply our way of trying to make life as easy as possible for you.

Of course, you can still get each of THE LOUD HOUSE graphic novels separately at your favorite booksellers. You can even get them digitally wherever e-books are sold – including at www.comiXology.com – if you prefer enjoying comics on your various digital devices. But if you're one of those completists, who absolutely must have each and every edition of THE LOUD HOUSE graphic novels, including second, third, and fourth printings, not to mention the mini-comic (which is re-presented on the following pages as a special bonus!) and the FREE COMIC BOOK DAY comic – we wish you luck! Trying to track down so many super-popular collector's item THE LOUD HOUSE graphic novels isn't easy! You could even say, "The Struggle is Real"! Collecting comics can be lots of fun – just ask Lincoln and Clyde – but we're trying to make getting THE LOUD HOUSE graphic novels as easy as possible. That's why you'll see THE LOUD HOUSE graphic novels popping up at more and more stores every day, not to mention book fairs, and even a few unexpected places.

Which is our cue, to remind that coming soon to a bookseller near you (possibly even at Flip's Food and Fuel, but be careful not to spill your Flippee on it!) is THE LOUD HOUSE #8 "Livin' la Casa Loud"! Not only will it feature all sorts of great comics starring your favorite characters from THE LOUD HOUSE, there's a very good chance there'll also be a Watch Out for Papercutz page with news about THE LOUD HOUSE #9! And we're sure you won't want to miss that!

Thanks,

Jim

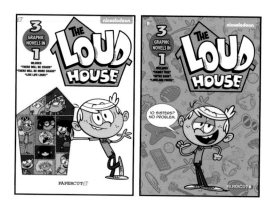

STAY IN TOUCH!

EMAIL: salicrup@papercutz.com
WEB: papercutz.com
TWITTER: @papercutzgn
INSTAGRAM: @papercutzgn
FACEBOOK: PAPERCUTZGRAPHICNOVELS
FANMAIL: Papercutz, 160 Broadway, Suite 700, East Wing, New York, NY 10038

"DEUCES WILD"

THE HIGH CARD

THE 11 OF HEARTS

NIGHT CLUBS

THE JOKER

STRONG SUIT

EIGHT OF SPADES

ROYAL FLUSH

QUEEN OF DIAMONDS

CARD COUNTER

64

LUCY (8)

CLYDE (11)

LINCOLN (11)

LENI (16)

LORI (17)

BOBBY (17)

LILY (15 mos)   LISA (4)   LOLA (6)   LANA

LYNN (13)   LUAN (14)   LUNA (15)